Otis

AND THE Kittens

D0131548

AND THE Kittens
LOREN LONG

PHILOMEL BOOKS

It was hot and dry on the farm where the friendly little tractor named Otis lived.

Otis couldn't remember the last time it had rained. Farmers all over the valley grew more anxious by the day. Water was in short supply, the ground was hard, and the cornstalks were half as tall as they should've been.

Otis spent his afternoons out in the sweltering fields with the farmhands baling straw.

Once the load was full, with a *puff* and a *chuff*, Otis
would pull the wagon into the old barn down by the bend
at Mud Creek.

The farmhands would use a pulley to lift each bale up into
the loft, where it would be stored for the long winter to come.

When the sun had gone over the hill and work was done,
Otis was ready to sit in the shade and rest.

But not Otis's friend the bull . . .

The bull liked to stand in front of Otis and snort and snarl and huff hot air.
Two snorts, a snarl, and a huff!

All the animals knew what that meant . . . the bull was challenging Otis to
a tug-of-war! Otis smiled. His friends were always eager to play, even after a
long day of work.

One duck wound the end of a rope around the bull's horns. Another duck looped the other end around Otis's steering wheel. The animals then took sides, grabbing on any way they could.

Everyone pulled and tugged with all of their might.

Eventually, Otis would ease up a little. He didn't care much about winning. He just liked having fun with his friends.

One afternoon when everyone was up under the shade of the apple tree, Otis spotted something moving down in the field. It looked to be an orange tabby cat! Where did she come from? Otis wondered. He watched as she ran toward the old barn, and there he saw something that caused his engine to sputter . . . a swirl of smoke!

Otis raced to the barn with the animals following behind. They discovered flames coming from the loft inside the old barn. A fire! The barn was filled with brittle, dry straw, and Otis knew it wouldn't take long for it all to burst into flames.

Just then, the tabby cat appeared in the barn window.

With a *putt puff puttedy chuff*, Otis rushed into the burning barn.

Inside, the flames were growing and smoke was forming a dark cloud.

The cat was pacing back and forth high above on a rafter.

Otis *chuff*ed for her to jump down, but the cat wouldn't budge. Instead, she stared down at Otis and belted out the loudest meow Otis had ever heard.

What was she trying to tell him?

Suddenly, Otis heard a tiny meow from the hayloft. And then another tiny meow and another and another and another and another. At once, five furry little heads popped up and stared down at him. Kittens!

As flames blazed overhead, Otis stood on hind wheels and stretched to the edge of the loft. To a chorus of tiny meows, one by one, the kittens hopped down.

The farm animals cheered as Otis emerged from the burning
barn with kittens all over him.

But as soon as mama cat counted their little heads, she meowed frantically back at the barn. This time, Otis had no doubt what she was saying. How many more were still in there? he wondered.

By then, the top of the barn was engulfed in flames, sending large plumes of smoke into the sky.

Otis was afraid, but he gunned his engine, screeched his tires, and dashed back into the burning barn.

Inside, the heat was growing worse and it was hard to breathe. Otis revved
his engine, and one last little head popped up, trembling from fear. Otis
puffed a gentle *chuff* and the kitten climbed down on top of him, hopped to
his seat, leapt to the floor, and scampered out of the barn to safety.

Outside, the animals cheered when they saw another kitten emerge. And they watched for Otis to follow.

Inside, the flames spread by the second.

Otis wheeled around to see if any more kittens were left. The old boards of the barn's floor creaked, buckled, and moaned. The walls popped. He couldn't wait another second.

Just as Otis spotted the exit and raced his wheels to leave, there was a giant CRASH!

The floor collapsed and Otis plunged to the darkness below.

Outside, the animals held their breath, waiting for their friend to emerge.

Inside, Otis couldn't move.

He had fallen into the cluttered lower level of the old barn. And he was covered in dust, debris, and broken planks.

Stuck in the hole with the fire raging above, Otis could hardly *puff* a breath.

Then he heard the siren of Fire Chief Douglas and the fire engine.
The farmer pulled up and Otis heard him rounding up the animals. Help
had arrived!

He knew he'd be fine, until he heard Fire Chief Douglas holler . . .

"Sorry, farmer, the creek's gone dry in the drought and the water supply's too low to save this old barn! As long as everyone's safe, we'll have to let 'er burn!"

Underneath the pile of broken boards and dust, Otis couldn't see a thing or move a gasket, and his heart sank deep inside his engine.

The animals had grown wild with fear.

The farmer counted them one by one. They were all safe and sound. He couldn't figure out why they were acting so crazy.

Suddenly, the little calf bolted for the barn door.
Her friends followed right behind.

Inside the fiery barn, they spotted Otis stuck down in the hole,
covered in boards and dust. His engine was barely running.

How could they ever get him out?

The bull looked up at the rafters and down at Otis.

He stood in front of the hole in the floor and snorted and snarled and huffed hot air.

Two snorts, a snarl, and a huff!

The animals knew just what that meant.

One duck grabbed the pulley rope and wound it around the bull's horns. Another duck flew into the hole and hooked it to Otis's steering wheel.

The bull snorted and tugged and snarled and pulled, but Otis didn't budge.

The horse and the cow grabbed the rope behind the bull and together they snorted and tugged and neighed and mooed and pulled, and Otis teetered ever so slightly. The little calf jumped in and tugged and bawled and pulled, and Otis raised a bit more.

The puppy grabbed the rope behind the little calf and with a fierce *arrhf*
tugged and pulled and growled as Otis inched upward.

And then came a piercing meow and the sound of Fire Chief Douglas shouting,
"Holy moly! Otis is in there! Hold on tight, everyone, I'm here to help!"

Fire Chief Douglas grabbed the end of the rope and tugged
and pulled and tugged. All together, the animals and Fire Chief
Douglas lifted Otis higher and higher, until he was suspended
above the hole.

The ducks swooped in and pushed him over the edge of the
opening to where they could lower him to the floor.

Together everyone pulled the dust- and ash-covered tractor
out from the burning fire just as parts of the barn began to fall.

Then Fire Chief Douglas and his men hosed off Otis and wiped down his frame. The cool water revived Otis, and everyone cheered when they heard a faint *putt puff puttedy chuff.* It was music to their ears.

The kittens jumped up on top of Otis and crawled all over him.

Fire Chief Douglas laughed and said, "Farmer, what say we adopt these kittens and their mama? They'd make a mighty fine addition to our firehouse family!"

Otis puffed a happy *chuff.* He couldn't think of a better home for his new friends.

THE END

OTHER BOOKS IN THE OTIS SERIES:

Otis

Otis and the Tornado

Otis and the Puppy

Otis Loves to Play

An Otis Christmas

and

Otis and the Scarecrow

PHILOMEL BOOKS an imprint of Penguin Random House LLC
375 Hudson Street, New York, NY 10014

Philomel Books is a registered trademark of Penguin Random House LLC.

Library of Congress Cataloging-in-Publication Data
Names: Long, Loren, author, illustrator. | Title: Otis and the kittens / Loren Long. | Description: New York, NY : Philomel Books, [2016] | Summary: When Otis the tractor becomes trapped in a burning barn, after rescuing kittens, his animal friends and local firefighters come to his aid. | Identifiers: LCCN 2016002362 | ISBN 9780399163982 (hardback) | Subjects: | CYAC: Tractors—Fiction. | Fires—Fiction. | Fire fighters—Fiction. | Domestic animals—Fiction. | Farm life—Fiction. | BISAC: JUVENILE FICTION / Animals / Farm Animals. | JUVENILE FICTION / Lifestyles / Farm & Ranch Life. | JUVENILE FICTION / Social Issues / Friendship. | Classification: LCC PZ7.L8555 Otk 2016 | DDC [E]—dc23 | LC record available at https://lccn.loc.gov/2016002362
Manufactured in China by RR Donnelley Asia Printing Solutions Ltd.
ISBN 9780399163982
Special Markets ISBN 9781524738778
10 9 8 7 6 5 4 3 2 1
Edited by Michael Green.   Design by Semadar Megged.   Text set in 15.5-point Engine.
The art was created in gouache and pencil.